D1403934

Feet Man
and
Mr. Tiny

Gina Freschet

Farrar Straus Giroux
New York

For my siblings:
Leslie, Dinah, Maria,
and Frank

Copyright © 2006 by Gina Freschet
All rights reserved
Distributed in Canada by Douglas & McIntyre Ltd.
Color separations by Chroma Graphics PTE Ltd.
Printed and bound in the United States of America by Phoenix Color Corporation
Designed by Jay Colvin
First edition, 2006
1 3 5 7 9 10 8 6 4 2

www.fsgkidsbooks.com

Library of Congress Cataloging-in-Publication Data
Freschet, Gina.
    Feet Man and Mr. Tiny / Gina Freschet.— 1st ed.
        p.   cm.
    Summary: After Feet Man, who is tired of people disparaging
his barge-sized feet, meets Mr. Tiny, the two of them set out to
find Feet Man's true calling.
    ISBN-13: 978-0-374-32294-6
    ISBN-10: 0-374-32294-5
    [1. Self-esteem—Fiction.   2. Foot—Fiction.   3. Size—Fiction.
4. Prejudices—Fiction.]   I. Title.

PZ7.F88968 Fe 2006
[E]—dc22

                                                    2004061525

Feet Man woke up early because his feet were cold. They stuck way out of the blankets. His foot size was triple-extra-umpteen-large. Each one was as big as a barge.

He used two bars of soap every day—one for each foot. The soap slivers left over he used for the rest of him. Keeping clean was exhausting.

No shoes fit him, so he had to go barefoot. When he walked,
his steps sounded like oars hitting water: *Slap, slap, slap!*

Feet Man was shy around people and seldom spoke. When he tried to be social, someone would joke, "There he goes, putting his foot in his mouth again." It happened today. And everybody laughed as usual.

"He's always off on the wrong foot!" More laughter.

"Careful, he might stand up for himself!"
"Or he might put his foot down!"
They giggled and guffawed, chuckled and chortled.
Feet Man muttered, "Put a sock in it." But no one heard him.

"I'm sick of these blimps I have to walk on!" he said to himself. "These feet are good for nothing. I'm tired of being made fun of. I wish I could show those guys I'm just as good as they are."

Suddenly, Feet Man felt a powerful itch. He sat down to scratch it when a voice cried out, "Help!" And there, wedged between two digits, was a little man. He was about the size of Feet Man's big piggy. "Help!"

Feet Man pried him out and the tiny man yelped, "Why don'tcha watch where you're going?"

"My feet are so big that I can't see the ground."

"They *are* pretty huge."

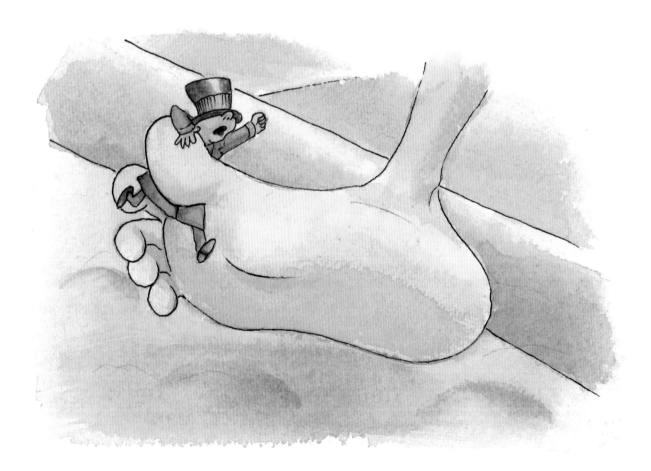

"Yes," Feet Man sighed. "I'm Feet Man. But people call me
Bigfoot and Clodhopper. Everyone makes fun of me."

"Me, too," said the small man. "Me, too. People call me the Teeny Tot of Tiny Town, Dinky Drip, and Micro Chip. But my real name's Mr. Tiny. And the little life has its shortcomings, too. I'm often mistook for a bug. I was once lost for a day under a rug."

He brushed himself off.

"But I just brush it all off. Because being small also has its advantages. I can see without being seen. I can travel very light. I've been around the world disguised as a kola nut and a coffee bean."

Looking sadly at his toes, Feet Man answered, "Not me. No advantages. I travel very heavy."

Mr. Tiny told him, "What you are, my friend, is unusual. And for that there is always a use. I'm sure you have talent. You just need a little encouragement."

"You think?"

"You're talkin' to the expert," Mr. Tiny told him. "How's about you and me pal around?"

Feet Man brightened. "Want to come over to my place?"

"Let's hoof it."

Together, they set off. *Slap, slap, slap!* Mr. Tiny choked on dust until Feet Man picked him up, put him in his pocket, and carried him the rest of the way home.

When they arrived, Mr. Tiny said, "Now, let's get some shut-eye, Feet Man, 'cause tomorrow we're gonna find you a use."

That night Mr. Tiny slept in Feet Man's spoon rest.

And the next morning at breakfast, Mr. Tiny announced, "It's a brand-new day. Time to go get 'em, big guy. Let's look at today's paper and see what's doin'."

Feet Man brought him the newspaper. "I've always wondered if I could be a dancer," he uttered shyly.

"Hmm. I'm skeptical, Feet Man. Anyways, there aren't any jobs for dancers today." Then he spied something.

"Look here at this advertisement," Mr. Tiny said. "The Husky Puppy Shoe Company claims: 'We Can Fit Any Foot. If We Can't Fit Your Size, We'll Give You a Giant Prize.'"

Mr. Tiny looked up at Feet Man. "It's perfect! A cakewalk, a walk in the park."

"It is?"

"But of course!"

"Are you *sure*?"

"Would I *lie?* With dogs like yours, you're a *shoe*-in to win. Hey—the contest's today, so let's step on it!"

On the way to the shoe store, Mr. Tiny gave tons of encouragement. "When we get there, take it one step at a time, put your best foot forward, stay on your toes, keep your feet on the ground, no fancy footwork, just toe the line, and you'll be fine."

Feet Man didn't know how to heed all of this advice at once. "I'll try," he said.

At the Husky Puppy Shoe Company, many other contestants had gathered. There were lots of feet.
Gigantic feet, titanic feet,
humungous feet and fungus feet.

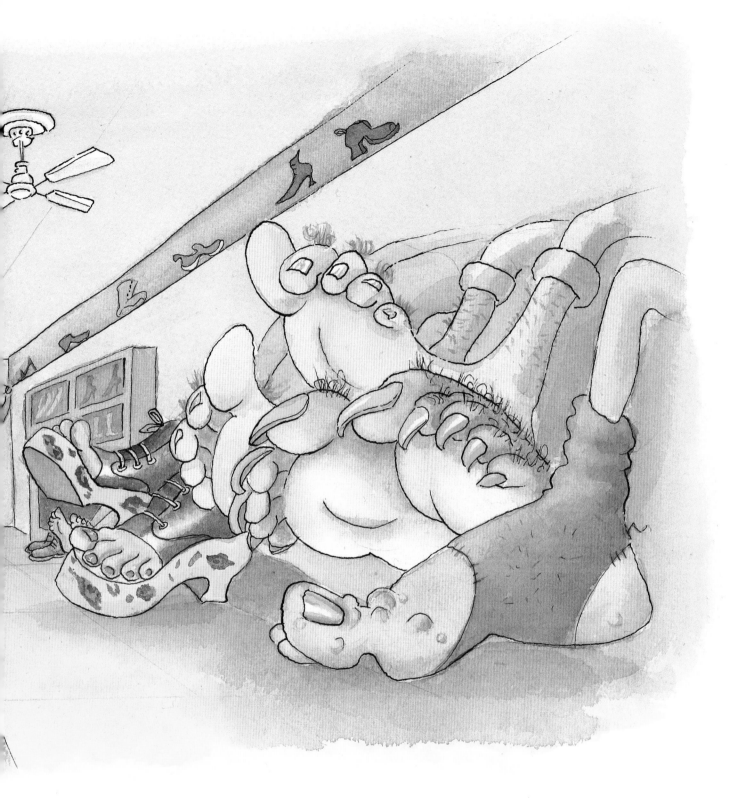

Stubby feet, grubby feet, horny feet and corny feet.
Fat feet, flat feet, square feet and bare feet,
very, very hairy feet and absolutely scary feet.

But there was a pair of shoes to fit every contestant except Feet Man.

When they gave him his trophy, Feet Man said, "Wow! I've never been a winner before. What a kick!" And he did a little jig.

People moved out of the way.

The giant prize was a trip to Florida. Mr. Tiny went along in the pocket of Feet Man's Hawaiian shirt. "This is great," he said. "Now we can cool our heels and relax."

Feet Man had never been to the beach before. When he stepped in the ocean, his feet were so big, so broad, so buoyant —he walked right across the water: *Slap, slap, slap!*

Mr. Tiny exclaimed, "Now *that's* talent!"

People crowded to see. They were very impressed.

Feet Man had a sudden inspiration.

He decided to try out his favorite dances, which he'd been practicing in secret for years—on the water.

He did . . .

the Flying Buttress,

the Rockette,

the Jumping Jack Splash,

the Ode to a Shrunken Bush.

He did the Monster Mash,

the Dying Swan,

the Funky Monkey,

and the Fabulous Finale.

The huge audience that had gathered roared with approval.
They gave Feet Man a big hand, which was exciting for
someone who'd only ever known big feet.

"I knew there was something special about you, and that with a little encouragement we'd find it," said Mr. Tiny.
Feet Man felt quite proud.

There was another advantage to having big feet. They were
wonderful for tickling. And Mr. Tiny was handy with a feather.
And there is nothing so good as laughter.

Washington County Free Library
100 South Potomac Street
Hagerstown, MD 21740-5504
www.washcolibrary.org

7450444